THE PROCESSION

TO MY MOTHER AND FATHER.

The Procession

by

MARGARET MAHY

pictures by

CHARLES MOZLEY

Franklin Watts, Inc.

575 Lexington Avenue · New York, N. Y. 10022

watts
INTERNATIONAL

Text and illustrations copyright © 1969 Franklin Watts, Inc.
Published in the United States by Franklin Watts, Inc.,
and in Great Britain by J. M. Dent & Sons Ltd.
Library of Congress Catalog Card Number: 69-19588
Printed in Austria

Who came tapping at the door? A wild, wandering man, green as Spring! Who came running to open the door? A little girl, eight years old, dressed in a filmy, floating, cloudy nightgown!

"Will you dance around the world with me?" said the wandering fellow.

"Yes, of course I'll come," said the little girl. Off they went together into a primrose-pale morning. The wanderer played his violin and they danced along the road.

Who was it who knocked at the door? A wild, wandering man and a little girl wearing a filmy, cloudy gown.

Who came running to open the door? A man with great gray bird wings growing from his shoulders!

"Will you come dancing with us?" they asked him.

"I have been waiting for you," he told them. "Why were you so long in coming for me?"

Off they went together into a rose crystal morning. They danced along the road. The wanderer played his violin, and the little girl sang:

"Honey, honey, dripping from the flower,
Petals, petals, falling from the rose,
Where can I find yesterday's happy hour?
No one knows! Nobody knows!"

Who came tapping at the door? A wild, wandering fellow, a little girl in a filmy, flowing gown, and a man with bird wings.

Who came running to open the door? A fiery man and his friend the dragon!

"Will you come with us?" they asked.

"Can my dragon come, too?"

"Yes, we need a dragon."

"Well, then, I will come as far as you are going."

Off they went, and then suddenly it was lunch-time.

"Will you have pepper in your stew?" the wandering fellow asked politely.

"Will you have honey on your bread, or cheese?" asked the bird-winged man. They toasted muffins on the dragon's breath, and drank lemonade.

"Do you know what we are?" asked the little girl happily. "We are a Procession!"

"There are no trumpets—" the dragon pointed out doubtfully.

"The happy feelings inside us are the trumpets for our Procession," the fiery man replied peacefully.

The Procession went on . . . . through a wood, . . .

over a bridge. . . .

across the sea in little boats with bright sails like gay wings,

over the water. . . .

over a desert, on silent, proud camels. . . .

up a sharp mountain that was like a tooth biting at the sky.

The Procession came up to the castle where the
young King was kept with five schoolmasters to
read him books on law and government, and five
guards to make sure nothing disturbed him.

Who was it who clanged on the bell at the Castle gate? The Procession! Who came running to peer through the window bars? The young King, wild in his crimson robes, shining like a rose-red star.

"Take me with you!" he cried. "I want to see, and hear, and feel, the wide world outside."

Who came running to pull the young King away from the bars?

Five guards, and five wise men in dark cloaks
like learned umbrellas, frayed at the edges.

"Law is a fine thing, and government a fine long word," said the wandering fellow, "but what of the song at night by the fire? A King should hear this, once in his life."

"Come back to your books on law and government," the five schoolmasters begged the young King, "or you will never learn enough to rule as a King!"

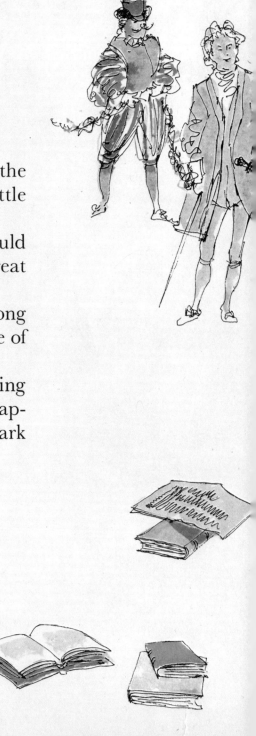

"A King should dance in the moon, and feel the black and silver night around him," said the little girl.

"Oh," said the bird-winged man, "a King should know poetry that sings, like the soaring of great feathered wings."

"A King should feel in his heart that life is strong as the music of trumpets, and warm as the flame of a dragon," added the fiery man.

And the dragon ended: "But not only a King should know these things. A guard with his weapons should know them, and a wise man in a dark cloak should know about them, too."

So the guards opened the gate
and the young King ran out.

The wise men followed him, flinging off their dark cloaks.
Underneath they wore gay patchwork, like five pied pipers.

The guards left their weapons to rust, and went out dressed in brown and green, like five sturdy trees.

"Now we are a *real* Procession!" said the little girl.

"But no trumpets!" complained the bird-winged man.

"The happiness we feel is like trumpets," the five wise men said.

"Or like kettle drums!" said the five guards.

"It is all sorts of music," said the young King.

The Procession went on and on with singing and dancing and being happy.

Perhaps tomorrow they will knock at *your* door!

Five Fairy Tale Princesses
Book and Charm Bracelet

Cinderella

The Princess and the Pea

Rapunzel

Sleeping Beauty

Snow White

by Berthe Amoss

Random House 🏠 New York

Manufactured in China 10 9 8 7 6 5 4 3 2 1
http://www.randomhouse.com/kids/

Cinderella

Once there was a man who had a lovely daughter named Ella. Ella's mother died when she was very young, and her father married again, this time to a mean woman with two daughters exactly like herself. Soon after his wedding, Ella's father also died, leaving Ella at the mercy of her jealous stepsisters and selfish stepmother. They gave Ella all the chores to do.

The stepsisters dressed in the latest fashion, but Ella had nothing but rags to wear. They called her Cinder-Ella because she had to sit in the cinders by the chimney to stay warm.

Now, it happened that the king's son invited all the young ladies of the land to a ball so that he could choose one to be his bride. Cinderella's stepsisters were so excited they thought of nothing else. They made Cinderella stay up every night sewing a marvelous ball gown for each of them.

The night of the ball, Cinderella curled their hair, laced their corsets, ironed their petticoats, and buttoned their gloves.

Then with their mother, the stepsisters climbed into their carriage and drove off, leaving Cinderella standing in a cloud of dust.

"How I wish I could go to the ball!" Cinderella said, watching until the carriage disappeared down the road.

"And so you shall!" came a voice from behind her.

Cinderella turned. There stood a beautiful lady with gossamer wings and a wand.

"I am your fairy godmother," she said. "Fetch me a pumpkin and two lizards from the garden and six mice and one large rat from the traps."

Cinderella did as she was told, her heart thumping with excitement. When the fairy godmother waved her magic wand, the pumpkin became a golden carriage, the lizards turned into footmen dressed in velvet, the mice became a team of magnificent snow-white horses, and the rat changed into a dapper coachman.

"Now it is your turn," said the fairy godmother as she turned Cinderella's rags into a sparkling ball gown, with glass slippers to match. "Off you go!" she said. "But don't forget—at midnight the magic will wear off, and your dress will turn back into rags and the coach into a pumpkin!"

Cinderella was by far the most beautiful young lady at the ball. She stole everyone's heart, including the heart of the prince, and he danced every dance with her. Cinderella was having such a wonderful time that she completely forgot her fairy godmother's warning. Then the clock began to strike twelve! Cinderella gave a little cry and ran from the prince's arms, out of the ballroom and down the palace stairs.

The prince ran after Cinderella, but all that he saw was a girl in rags running away and a single glass slipper twinkling on the palace steps.

The prince picked up the slipper and vowed he would find and marry the girl whose foot fit it.

The next day, the prince rode out into the kingdom to find his bride. When he arrived at Cinderella's house, each of the stepsisters struggled to force a foot into the dainty shoe, but neither could squeeze even one big toe into it.

"May I try?" asked Cinderella. Of course, the slipper fit perfectly because it was her very own!

Cinderella's fairy godmother appeared and waved her wand. Immediately, Cinderella was dressed in a beautiful gown. The two stepsisters recognized the beautiful princess from the ball and begged Cinderella for forgiveness. She forgave them because she had a generous heart, and after a magnificent wedding, they all lived happily together at the palace.

The Princess and the Pea

Once upon a time, there lived a prince who wished to marry a real princess, a girl who was brave, kind, and unselfish. So he traveled over the whole world in search of one. During his travels, he met many princesses, and while most were beautiful, they were often vain or greedy or mean-spirited. At last, the prince returned home to his castle, downcast and without a bride.

One evening, a dreadful storm gathered. Lightning crashed, thunder boomed, and rain poured down in torrents. Suddenly, a loud and urgent knocking was heard at the castle doors. The prince himself went out to see who was there. He pulled open the heavy door. There stood a young lady, dripping wet. The rainwater ran down from her hair, and her dress was drenched.

"Please, sir," she said, shivering. "My carriage has met with an accident and my coachman is in trouble. Please help him."

The prince brought her inside and sent people to help the coachman. The prince's mother, the old queen, ordered servants to start a fire and make a bed. But the girl would not move until she had been told that her coachman and horses were safe.

"She does not look like a real princess," thought the old queen, not saying a word. "But I know just how to find out."

When the mysterious girl went to her bedroom, she found that her bed was made up with twenty mattresses. They were piled so high that she had to climb a ladder to reach the top.

The next morning, the old queen saw circles under the girl's eyes. "You are a real princess," she said, smiling. "I can see you slept poorly. You felt the pea I hid under twenty mattresses. Only a real princess would be so sensitive."

The prince smiled too. He had seen from the first moment that the girl was beautiful, brave, and kind. He went down on his knee and asked her to marry him.

"I would be happy to be your wife," she replied. "Only a real prince would have opened the castle door on such a stormy night and helped a stranger in distress."

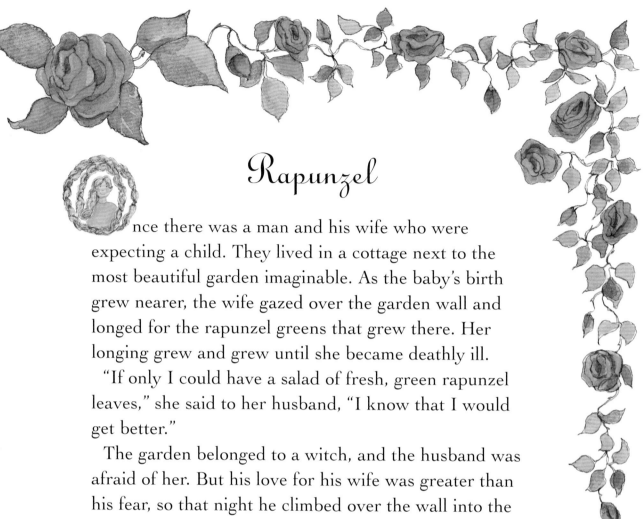

Rapunzel

nce there was a man and his wife who were
expecting a child. They lived in a cottage next to the
most beautiful garden imaginable. As the baby's birth
grew nearer, the wife gazed over the garden wall and
longed for the rapunzel greens that grew there. Her
longing grew and grew until she became deathly ill.

"If only I could have a salad of fresh, green rapunzel
leaves," she said to her husband, "I know that I would
get better."

The garden belonged to a witch, and the husband was
afraid of her. But his love for his wife was greater than
his fear, so that night he climbed over the wall into the
witch's garden and picked a handful of rapunzel leaves.
But one salad did not satisfy the wife, and the next
night the husband went back for more.

This time the witch was waiting for him. "Thief!" she
cackled. "You shall pay for this!"

The man explained about his wife's longing, but the
witch only laughed. "I will be generous," she said. "You
may have the rapunzel, but you must give me the child
you are expecting!"

The man had no choice. As soon as the baby girl was born, the witch appeared and snatched her away. The witch named the baby Rapunzel. Rapunzel grew into a lovely child, with silky, golden hair that was never cut. By the time she was sixteen, her hair was so long it reached past her feet.

About this time, the witch began to worry that her stolen daughter would escape. She took Rapunzel deep into the forest and imprisoned her in a tower that had no steps and no doors, only a small window at the top.

"Here you shall live, all alone and away from the world," said the witch.

The witch came often to bring food to Rapunzel. She would stand at the foot of the tower and call,

"*Rapunzel, Rapunzel,*
Let down your golden hair!"

Then Rapunzel would tie her braided hair to a hook on the window sill and let it drop to where the witch could reach it and climb up.

In her loneliness, Rapunzel began to sing to herself. One day, as she was singing a lovely melody, a prince passed by. The prince followed the music to the foot of the tower. He walked around and around looking for a door, and was about to give up when he spied the witch coming. The prince hid and heard the witch call out,

"*Rapunzel, Rapunzel,*
Let down your golden hair!"

As he watched, a braid of hair the color of sunlight fell from the tower window. The witch climbed up the braid.

"So that is how it is done!" thought the prince.

The next evening, he went to the tower and called,

"*Rapunzel, Rapunzel,*
Let down your golden hair!"

At once the thick braid of hair fell into his hands and he climbed into the tower. There, he beheld the most beautiful girl he had ever seen. Rapunzel was as enchanted as the prince, for he was very handsome, and as they talked, she saw that he was also kind and thoughtful.

"Will you be my wife?" the prince asked Rapunzel.

"Oh, yes," she answered. "You must bring me a skein of silk so that I can weave a ladder and run away with you."

The next day, the witch came to the tower and called to Rapunzel as usual.

Rapunzel was so full of dreams of love that as the witch was climbing, she said thoughtlessly, "How is it that you are so much heavier to pull up than the prince?"

The witch flew into a rage. She whipped out her scissors and cut off Rapunzel's hair. Then she took Rapunzel deeper into the forest and left her alone.

That night, it was the witch who let down Rapunzel's hair when the prince came calling. As he climbed into the tower, the witch laughed. "Your lovely little bride has flown away and you will never see her again!"

Wild with grief, the prince leaped from the tower. He fell into a thorny bush and was blinded. For many days, he wandered unseeing and uncaring through the forest until he heard a familiar voice singing.

"Rapunzel!" he cried.

Rapunzel rushed into his arms. Her tears of joy fell upon his eyelids and cured his blindness. Rapunzel and her prince made their way back to the prince's kingdom, where they lived happily ever after.

Sleeping Beauty

nce upon a time, a princess was born to a king and queen. They were so overjoyed that they named the lovely little girl Rose and invited seven good fairies to her christening.

After the christening ceremony, the fairies each gave a gift to Rose. The first gave her kindness, the next wit, then grace, charm, courage, and humor. Just as the sixth fairy had spoken, an evil fairy appeared in a dark cloud of smoke.

"Ha!" she cackled. "All the gifts in the world cannot save your little princess from my special present! " She leaned over Rose's crib. "On your sixteenth birthday, you will prick your finger on a spindle and die!" she cried. The wicked fairy pointed a long finger at the king and queen. "That's what you get for not inviting me to your little party!" And with a shriek of laughter, she disappeared in a puff of smoke.

"Alas, I cannot completely undo the evil fairy's curse," said the seventh fairy. "The princess shall indeed prick her finger on a spindle, but instead of dying, she shall fall asleep for one hundred years until a prince awakens her with a kiss."

Everyone in the kingdom grieved over little Rose's fate, and the king ordered all the spindles in the land burned. Soon, not a single one could be found. It was believed that the evil fairy's curse had been foiled forever.

The years rolled by and the danger was all but forgotten. Then on Rose's sixteenth birthday, while everyone was busy preparing for the party, the princess decided to explore the castle.

In her wanderings, she discovered a little door leading to a narrow staircase. Rose climbed the staircase to a tiny tower room. In the center sat the evil fairy, disguised as an old woman spinning. Rose had never seen a spindle before.

"What are you doing?" she asked.

"I am spinning, my pretty child," answered the wicked fairy. "Would you like to try?"

Rose reached out and touched the spindle. She cried out as a drop of blood appeared where the spindle had pricked her finger. Immediately, she fell to the floor, fast asleep.

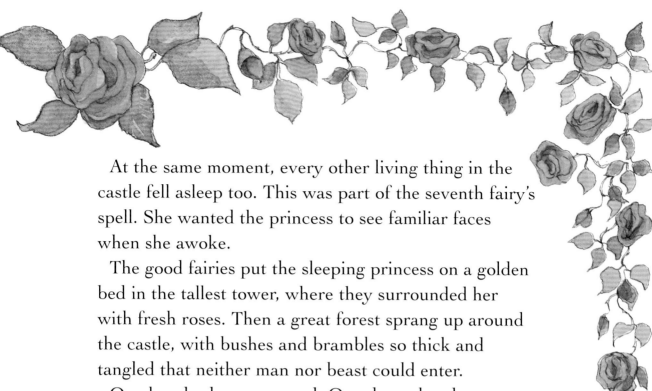

At the same moment, every other living thing in the castle fell asleep too. This was part of the seventh fairy's spell. She wanted the princess to see familiar faces when she awoke.

The good fairies put the sleeping princess on a golden bed in the tallest tower, where they surrounded her with fresh roses. Then a great forest sprang up around the castle, with bushes and brambles so thick and tangled that neither man nor beast could enter.

One hundred years passed. One day, a handsome prince was hunting nearby and saw the tower of a castle rising above the thick wood. As he rode toward it, the bushes and brambles parted to let him pass.

When the prince reached the castle, he saw men, women, and animals, all fast asleep. Filled with wonder, he followed a trail of roses to the tallest tower, where a golden door opened before him. There lay the beautiful princess amid a tangle of blooming roses.

The prince fell in love at first sight and kissed Rose's cheek. She opened her eyes. "It is you at last, my prince!" she said.

Just then, the king, the queen, and the whole court awoke, stretching and yawning. One by one they gathered around the happy couple. The sleeping beauty and her prince were married the very next day and lived happily ever after.

Snow White

Once upon a time, there lived a queen who wanted a child more than anything in the world. One winter's day, as she sat sewing by an ebony-framed window, she pricked her finger with the needle.

"Oh," she said, "if only I could have a little girl with skin as white as snow, lips as red as blood, and hair as black as ebony!"

In time, the queen's wish came true, and she named the baby Snow White.

Not long after, the queen died and the king married again. The new queen was beautiful but wicked and vain. Every night, she would gaze into a magic mirror and ask,

"Mirror, mirror, on the wall,
Who is the fairest of them all?"

And the mirror would reply,

"Queen, you are the fairest of
them all!"

But as time went on, Snow White grew ever lovelier, until one day the mirror answered,

"Queen, you are fair, 'tis true,
But Snow White is far more fair than you."

The queen was filled with jealousy. She ordered a hunter to take Snow White deep into the woods and kill her. But the hunter could not bear to hurt Snow White, and so he left her unharmed.

Terrified, Snow White ran through the forest until she came to a little cottage. She knocked on the door, but no one answered. She walked in and saw a little table with seven little chairs. Upstairs, Snow White found seven little beds, and being very tired, she lay down and fell fast asleep.

The cottage belonged to seven dwarfs who worked in a mine in the mountains close by. When they came home and found Snow White, they asked her to stay and keep house for them.

"Thank you, I would love to!" said Snow White.

That very night, the queen asked her mirror,

> *"Mirror, mirror, on the wall,*
> *Who is the fairest of them all?"*

The wicked queen was sure the mirror would tell her that she was once again the most beautiful. But the mirror answered,

> *"Queen, thou art fair, 'tis true,*
> *But over seven hills and far away,*
> *Snow White with seven dwarfs does stay,*
> *And she is far more fair than you!"*

The queen turned green with envy. She vowed to find a way to be rid of Snow White. Meanwhile, as she schemed, Snow White kept house for the dwarfs and grew even more beautiful.

One day, as Snow White was dusting, an old lady in ragged clothes knocked at the door.

"I'm sorry, but I cannot open the door," Snow White called. "The dwarfs told me not to let strangers in."

"Then come to the window, my dear," said the old lady. "You are such a pretty child that I shall give you a present."

Snow White opened the window. The old lady gave her an apple so red and beautiful that Snow White could not resist taking a bite. But when she did, she fell down as though dead. The old lady laughed wickedly, for it was the queen in disguise and she had poisoned the apple!

When the dwarfs returned and found Snow White, they wept for three days. They could not bear to bury her in the dark ground. Finally, they made a coffin of clear glass and placed it on top of the mountain.

One day, a prince riding by saw Snow White. He fell in love with her at first sight and begged the dwarfs to let him have the coffin. At last they consented, for they knew the prince loved Snow White.

As the prince's men carried the coffin to his palace, one stumbled over a root. The sudden motion shook loose the piece of poisonous apple that was lodged in Snow White's throat.

Snow White gave a little cough and opened her eyes. The first thing she saw was the handsome prince.

"Who are you?" she asked.

"The one who loves you," the prince replied joyfully, "and the one who would make you his bride!"

The wedding was the most splendid ever, and the dwarfs were there to give the bride away.

As for the wicked queen, the next time she asked the mirror,

> *"Mirror, mirror, on the wall,*
> *Who is the fairest of them all?"*

The mirror answered,

> *"Queen, you are a beauty rare,*
> *But Snow White, the bride,*
> *Is a thousand times more fair!"*

The queen flew into such a rage that she smashed the mirror and fell down dead.